For my grandparents and everything we left unsaid
(and for my editor, Rotem, who helps me find the right words) —M. L.

For my grandmother—D. S.

Text copyright © 2018 by Minh Lê
Illustrations copyright © 2018 by Dan Santat

All rights reserved. Published by Disney • Hyperion, an imprint of Disney Book Group. No part of this book may be reproduced or transmitted in any form or by any means, electronic or mechanical, including photocopying, recording, or by any information storage and retrieval system, without written permission from the publisher. For information address Disney • Hyperion, 125 West End Avenue, New York, New York 10023.

First Edition, June 2018 • 10 9 8 7 6 5 4 • FAC-029191-19236 • Printed in Malaysia • This book is set in Danvetica/Dan Santat; Futura LT Pro/ Monotype • Designed by Joann Hill • Illustrations created in traditional mixed media and composited on the computer • Library of Congress Cataloging-in-Publication Data • Names: Lê, Minh, 1979- author. • Santat, Dan, illustrator. • Title: Drawn together / by Minh Lê ; illustrations by Dan Santat. • Description: First edition. • Los Angeles ; New York : Disney-Hyperion, 2018. • Summary: A boy and his grandfather cross a language and cultural barrier using their shared love of art, storytelling, and fantasy. • Identifiers: LCCN 2016019315 • ISBN 9781484767603 (hardcover) • ISBN 1484767608 (hardcover) • Subjects: CYAC: Communication—Fiction. • Art—Fiction. • Storytelling—Fiction. • Grandfathers—Fiction. • Classification: LCC PZ7.1.L39 Dr 2018 • DDC [E]—dc23 • LC record available at https://lccn.loc.gov/2016019315 • ISBN 978-1-4847-6760-3 • Reinforced binding
Visit www.DisneyBooks.com

Thai text transcribed and translated by Nancy and Adam Santat.
The title page is page 5.
The text on page 9 means *How are you doing?*
The text on page 10 means *dragon.*
The text on page 11 means *Would you like to watch something else?*

drawn together

WRITTEN BY **MINH LÊ**

CALDECOTT MEDALIST
ILLUSTRATED BY **DAN SANTAT**

DISNEP • Hyperion

Los Angeles   New York

Right when I gave up on talking,

my grandfather surprised me
by revealing a world beyond words.

And in a FLASH—

we see each other for the first time.

But just when we're closer than ever,

that old distance...

...comes ROARING BACK.

Because I know that together

Now, after years of searching for the right words, we find ourselves happily...